Tyrannosaurus is pronounced: tie-ran-o-saw-rus

Lucy Anna Mary Wilson **KW**

Text copyright © Karen Wallace 2003
Illustrations copyright © Mike Bostock 2003

Designer: Sarah Borny

Consultant: Dr Angela Milner, Head of Fossil Vertebrates Division,
Department of Palaeontology, The Natural History Museum, London

First published in 2003
This paperback edition published in 2004
Reprinted in 2005

ISBN 0340 89385 0
Printed and bound in Hong Kong

Hodder Children's Books
A division of Hodder Headline Limited
338 Euston Road, London NW1 3BH

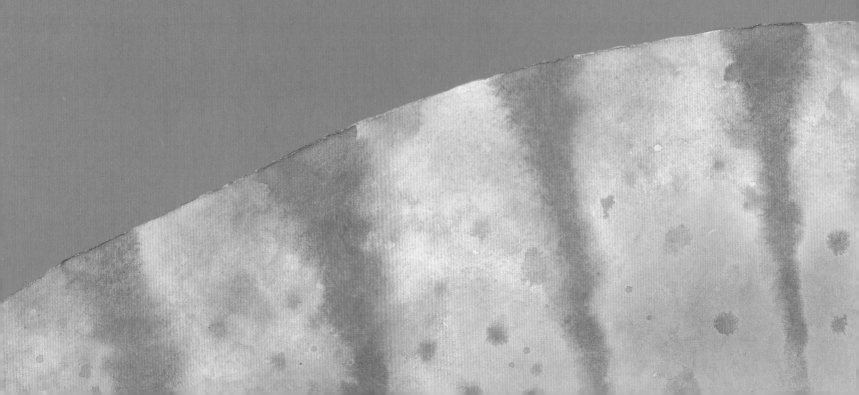

I am a Tyrannosaurus

Written by **Karen Wallace**

Illustrated by **Mike Bostock**

Hodder
Children's
Books

A division of Hodder Headline Limited

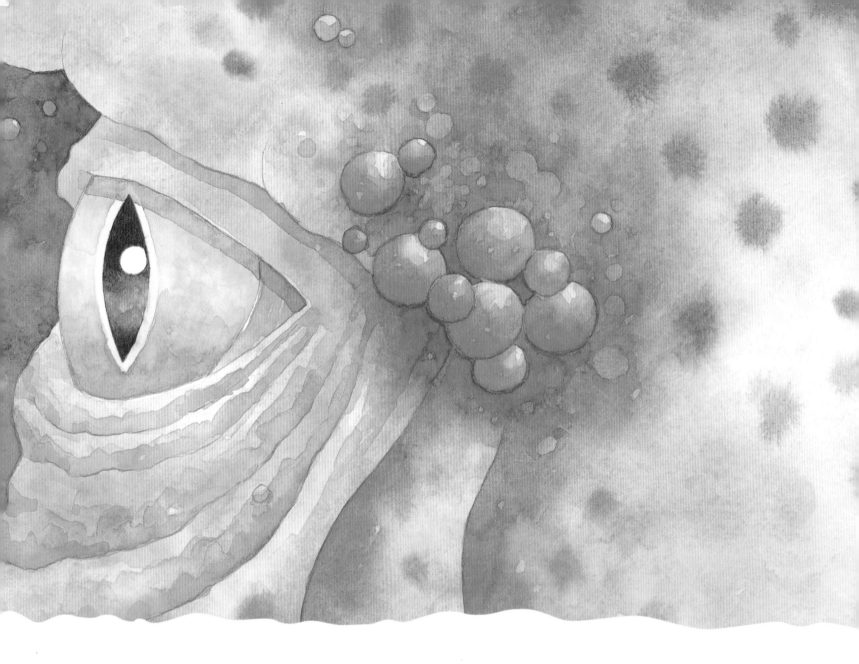

I am a tyrannosaurus.

I am prowling through the forest.

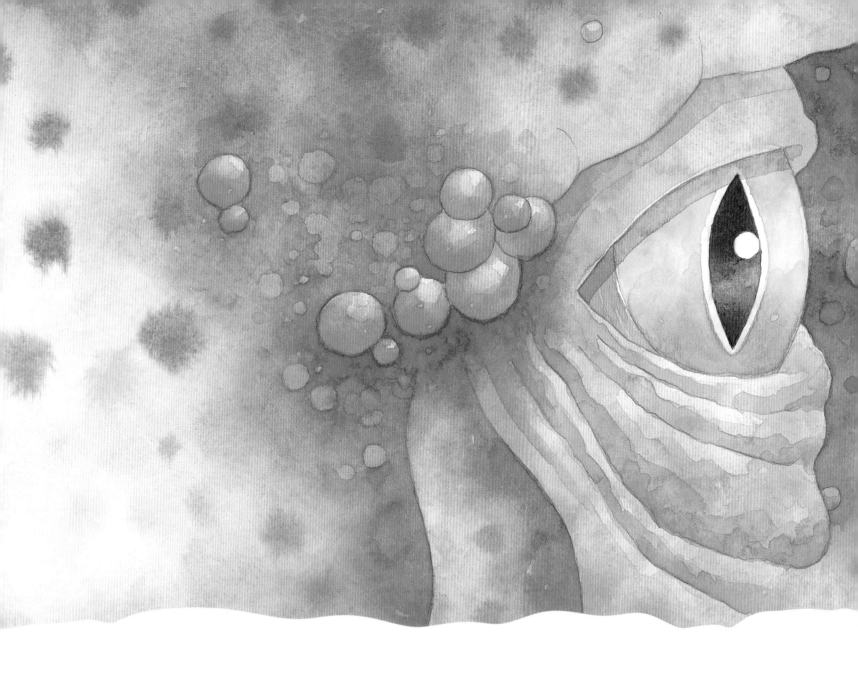

Look through my eyes and see what I see.

A thieving tyrannosaurus
prowls through a forest.
He has left his own
hunting ground.
He is hungry for meat.
He towers over trees.

He walks on his toes like a bird.
His claws make deep marks as
they sink in the ground.

A cunning tyrannosaurus
peers through the bushes.
A herd of triceratops is
grazing by a mud hole.
A sharp-eyed tyrannosaurus
picks out his victim.
A young triceratops
stands on his own.

The tyrannosaurus's teeth are curved and like daggers.

He opens his mouth as wide as he can.

As the triceratops turns to run,

the tyrannosaurus races towards him.

His teeth bite and slice.

His jaws shut like a trap.

Greedy tyrannosaurus!

He tears out great mouthfuls.

He holds down his prey with the claws on his feet.

As he crunches and gulps,
he looks all around him.
A bigger tyrannosaurus would chase him away.

The tyrannosaurus dozes.
His stomach is bloated.
He sleeps on flat rocks
that are warm in the sun.

A bright-feathered bird
calls in the branches
above him.

Dawn comes to the forest.
The sky is scarlet and gold.
The tyrannosaurus wakes.
He's still hungry for meat.
He heaves himself up on
his tiny front legs.

Wary tyrannosaurus!
He knows he's a thief in
this part of the forest.
He turns.
Another tyrannosaurus is
running towards him!

Two tyrannosaurus
stamp round in a circle.
They are hungry and angry.
Their jaws are wide open.
The triceratops's body lies
on the ground.
The stink of its carcass
hangs in the air.

Cowardly tyrannosaurus!
He won't fight for his food.
He runs back over the plains
to his own hunting ground.

Above him the sky is heavy and black.
Around him the air has turned
sour and strange.

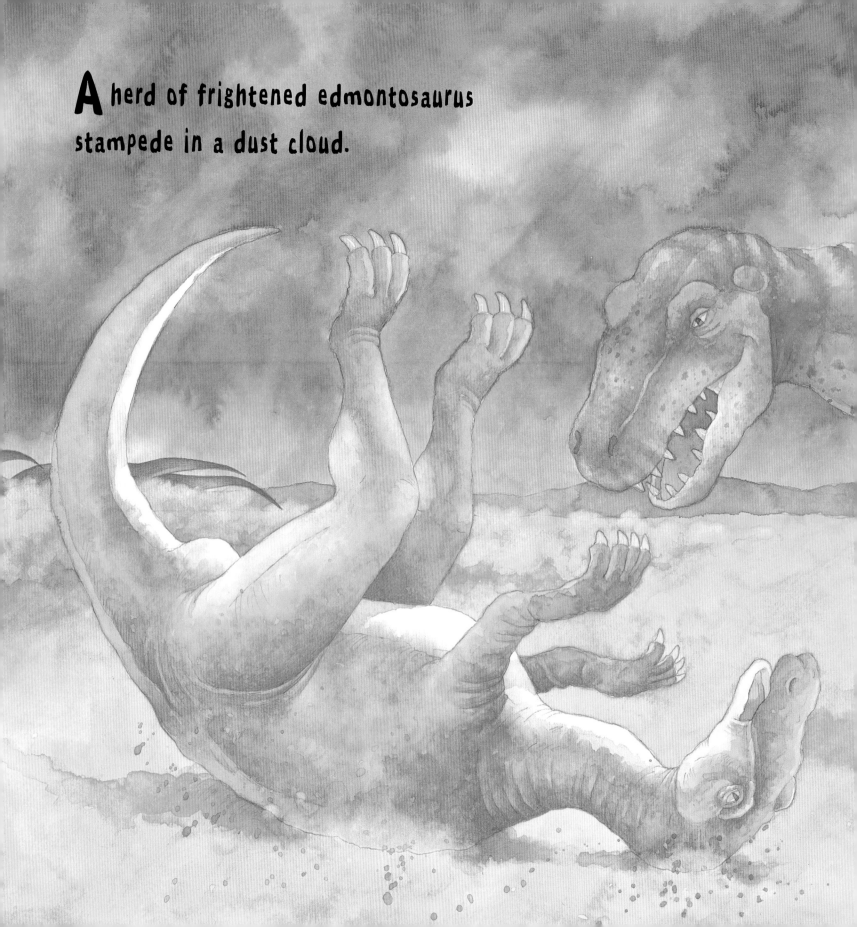

A herd of frightened edmontosaurus stampede in a dust cloud.

The air burns
like a furnace.
Chips of hot rock
swirl in the wind.
An edmontosaurus
stumbles.

**The
tyrannosaurus
attacks.**

I am a tyrannosaurus.

I slice through tough skin.
Dust swirls in my eyes.
Lumps like hot coals
crash down on my head.